Ollie's
Sketchbook

Ollie's Sketchbook

Suzy Naidoo

2017

First Printing: 2017

ISBN-13: 978-0-6482240-0-6

Published by Joyjoie Pty Ltd

Sydney, Australia

www.joyjoie.com.au

For Arianna, the most vigilant friend and daughter.
Always on the alert for gluten, nuts and eggs
while herself being allergy free.

Acknowledgments

Thank you to Anesan and Arianna for being excited to read the first draft for bed-time books and for continuing to be interested as edits turned into re-reads after re-reads.

Arianna also came up with the joke for this book as a bee spin on her ever unique versions of why did the chicken cross the road.

Ollie came to be because I love Arianna, Arianna loves bees, me (her mum) and her friends. I have intolerances and her friends have allergies. Living with food issues can be tough and alienating so I wanted to create a little world where allergies don't eclipse all the good in our lives even while they may be a big part of it.

My Sketchbook

February 21

This is me, Ollie...

TAG - never mind this for now it's new and I'm not really sure what it is

STINGER - don't worry I don't plan on using it

STRIPES - standard yellow and black

Today I went to the bee doctor, mum thinks I have allergies. It was kind of fun at first, they made me touch and sniff a whole heap of stuff...

We weren't even halfway through the pile of jars and bottles by lunchtime. It was kind of fun for me but mum was starting to get weird.

She was zooming around the room suggesting we try this and that. The doctor was fine at first but after the first 20 or so tests he asked mum if I had an exam coming up at school I was avoiding. I am not sure what exams have to do with allergies, I didn't realise you can be allergic to school?

Anyway, at this point mum, she started buzzing. This is never a good sign when I spilt honey all over mums jewellery box she started buzzing and made me clean it all with a toothbrush. Ever since then if I hear a buzz its time to find somewhere else to play.

The doctor must have noticed the buzz too, he gave me a look but I kept quiet, he was on his own to calm her down.

He must have decided avoiding the problem would be easiest and cleared off to have a snack.

I was starving and I knew mum had packed some 'Pollen Pop' which I couldn't wait to try. They are a mega treat and she never let me have them before.

Unfortunately, these did not turn out to be the treat for which I was hoping. Instead, I ended up toppling a stack of medical supplies as I zipped backwards with the force of my sneeze.

It must have been a pretty loud sneeze, the doctor and all the other bees at the clinic rushed into the room. It was chaos, mum was trying to pull me out of a pile of boxes. She had to be careful, stinger repair glue had squirted everywhere - I guess I punctured some containers - and I was kind of stuck in a box of the stuff.

3

I thought I would have been in trouble with mum about the mess - it was way worse than the honey in the jewellery box - but she gave me a big hug. Then in a triumphant voice asked the doctor to test me for pollen allergies.

This part was less fun.

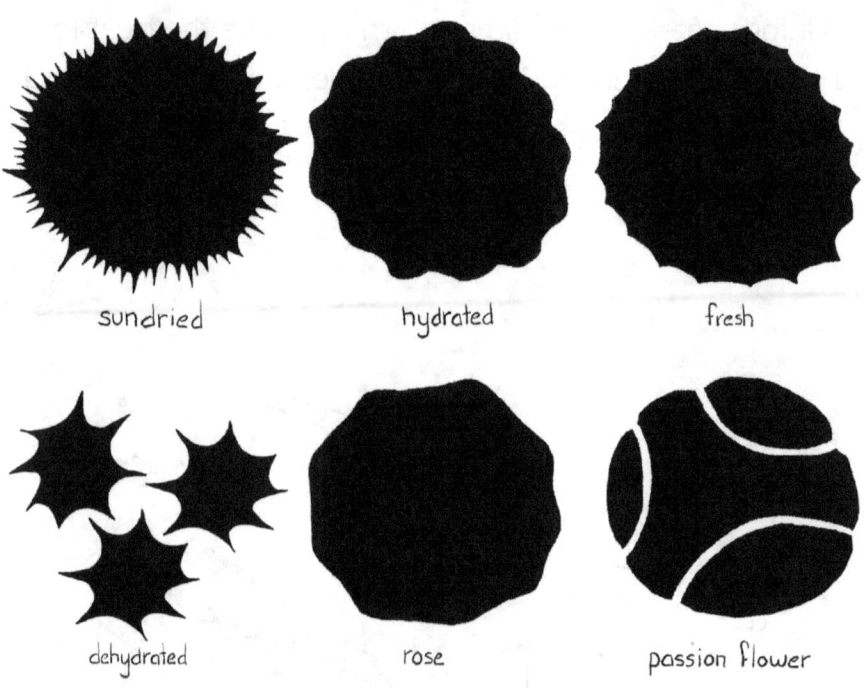

sundried

hydrated

fresh

dehydrated

rose

passion flower

They shoved all kinds of pollen in my face.

They made me smell pollen from all different types of flowers. I can't remember them all and I don't even think some of them grow around our lagoon but it didn't make any difference.

I sneezed at the rose pollen, swelled with the wattle pollen, shivered with the passion flower pollen, got all red and blotchy with the thyme pollen and itched with the Allium pollen.

I sneezed, swelled, spluttered and itched some more while they experimented with fresh pollen, sun-dried pollen, dehydrated pollen and hydrated pollen. What even is 'hydrated' pollen? All I could see was pollen floating in water and nectar.

After ages, the doctor said, "Ollie is to be completely 'Pollen Free' ". He said a whole heap more things to mum while I pretended to listen but I wasn't paying them much attention. The sneezes came so often I had no time to breathe and when I wasn't sneezing my six legs weren't enough to scratch all my itches. So how could I follow a conversation and deal with all that!

In the snippets of conversation, I did hear between sneezes the Doctor was explaining about a special diet, home pollen management and garden visits with a pollen collector to protect me.

Finally, they let us leave - me with a new dietary ID Tag and mum with a migraine. I didn't see them give her the migraine so I guess it's under all the papers and medicine we got.

February 22

So I guess this 'Pollen Free' thing is a pretty big deal. Mum has gone beyond buzzing level of upset, one minute she is all weepy and the next she is in a cleaning frenzy.

I'm still not sure why all the drama. I got to eat nectar for breakfast, lunch and dinner and I never had pollen before anyway, so its no big deal if I can't eat it. The only bad part is that they want me to keep a "food, activity and symptoms diary".

It seems pretty boring to me. I only eat nectar so what am I supposed to write about? Anyway, I've decided to make a sketchbook instead - this way I can draw anything I am not sure how to spell - but I'll tell mum it's because I want her to visualise (had to ask her how to spell that) what I am writing about.

February 23

Breakfast – Nectar

Activity – Watched mum dust the compartment.

Lunch – Nectar

Activity – Watched mum clean out the air filters.

Dinner – Nectar

Activity – This is it, filling out my journal.

Symptoms – Mild boredom.

February 24

Breakfast – Nectar

Activity – Watched mum clear out all the jars of pollen from the kitchen.

Lunch – Nectar

Activity – Watched mum dust the compartment.

Dinner – Nectar

Activity – Filling out my journal.

Symptoms – Mild boredom with a touch of want to go outside.

February 25

Breakfast – Nectar

Activity – Went outside which should have been good but wasn't.

Lunch – Nectar

Activity – Watched mum dust the compartment again.

Dinner – Nectar

Activity – Filling out my journal and thinking about how I can convince mum to never make me go out with the pollen collector again.

Symptoms - Severe irritation, the pollen collector that took me outside wouldn't let me fly around. I might just as well have stayed home to watch mum spray the compartment with an anti-pollen static solution, it would have been more fun.

He made me hover right by the hive with him right in front of me, I couldn't even see past him. Plus, he was in a bad mood, grumbling about wasting prime pollen collecting conditions and having to be decontaminated just to babysit.

Actually, it did sound pretty bad. They made him go into a supercharged static compartment – pollen is attracted to static so it basically pulled the stuff away from him - and it kept zapping him. He had to stay in there for ages and now he has a bit of a twitch in his wings.

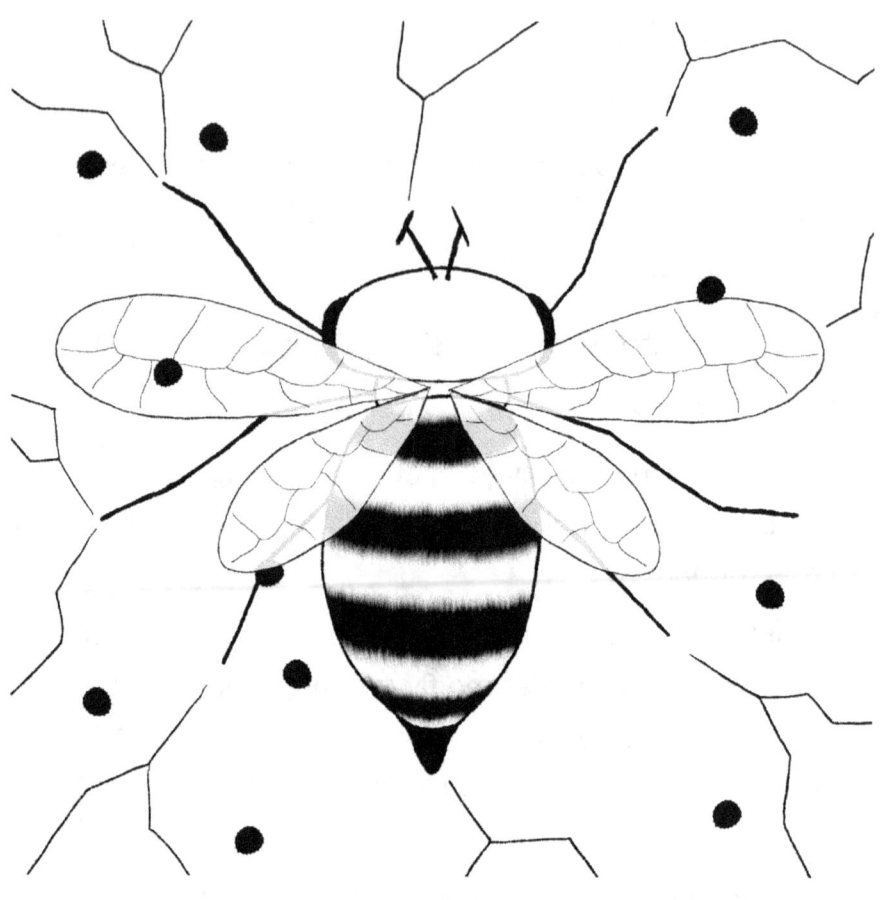

February 26

Breakfast – Nectar

Activity – Mum cleaning.

Lunch – Nectar

Activity – Stared at the ceiling.

Dinner – Nectar

Activity – Had to calm mum down, she heard from the pollen collector today. He says he won't take me outside anymore, apparently, I have ruined his chance of winning the annual pollen collection award at this year's winter gala. At least I won't have to listen to him grumbling or spend any more time staring at his back.

Symptoms – Boredom

February 27

Breakfast – Nectar

Activity – Slept

Lunch – Nectar

Activity – Mum cleaning.

Dinner – Nectar

Activity – Filling out my journal.

Symptoms – Extreme boredom.

February 28

Breakfast – Nectar

Activity – Helped mum clean the filters again she said it was about time I stopped staring at the ceiling.

Lunch – Nectar

Activity – Yep, more cleaning.

Dinner – Nectar

Activity – Filling out my journal.

Symptoms – There is nothing to do in here, I am so bored!!!

March...

Nothing new to report, still eating nectar, still sitting around the compartment.

VERY bored.

April 1

Today was brilliant.

The hive is all upset about the low pollen count but as soon as mum heard she had me out the door and in the sunshine before I even had a chance to wake up. All this time she's been faking that it's fine being stuck in the compartment cleaning.

We didn't even care when it started to rain, we relaxed out under a big leaf and told each other bad jokes.

This was my favourite...

"Why did the bee cross the stream?"

"I don't know, why?"

"Because bees don't know how to read the signs."

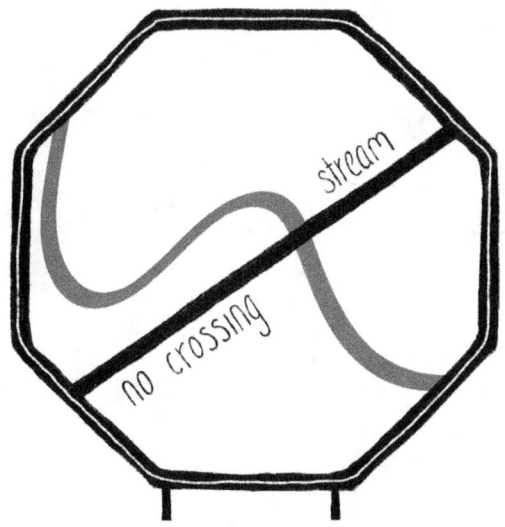

We had a bit of a close call with some pollen on the way back to the hive, mum freaked out but I did a cool aerial loop right around it.

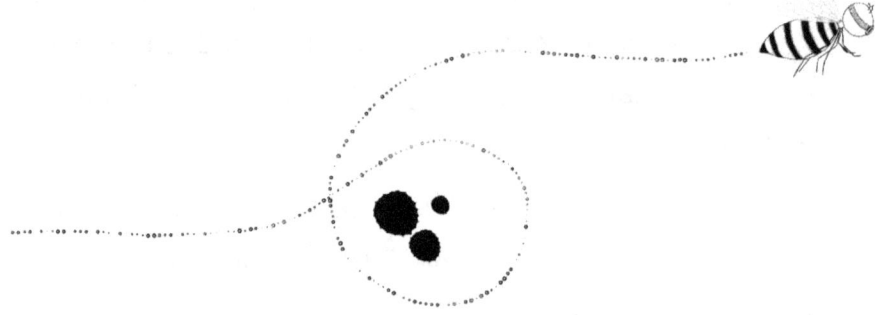

My antennae didn't even catch a twitch.

I hope tomorrow will be another low pollen count day.

April 2

No good, the pollen count exploded today. The wind was blowing the stuff everywhere. Mum had to clean the pollen filters four times and she went through a whole bottle of anti-pollen static spray.

April 3

Another bad day, now mum has stopped pretending to like being inside too and it's miserable. All we had to do was clean. But there is only so much cleaning we can do so, even worse, Mum decided I needed to practice my reading. All we had to read was the vacuum cleaner maintenance manual and it was worse than the time she made me read "Hive Living".

I am not fooled, she wants me to start using more words in my sketchbook.

April 4

I'm getting Pollen Detection Goggles! I read about them in today's newspaper – mum let me read that instead of the vacuum cleaner manual which was so blah.

DAILY BEE

4 April 2017

April Fools Day Prank Woes

Bees in Lagoon Park Hive were served with a honey production warning today.

In an exclusive statement to Daily Bee, the Minister for Honey reported that a record drop in honey production precipitated this unprecedented action by the Department for Honey.

The full details of the cause for the decline in honey production have yet to come to light but an anonymous source from the hive in question has

indicated that an April Fools day prank may have been taken too far.

According to our source a hive-wide holiday was declared on the morning of April 1st, 2017 following a report to the Queen of a low pollen count in the Lagoon Park local area.

Officials from the Lagoon Park Hive have declined to comment however this reporter has observed a gre...

of pollen collec...

the pr...

Scient:

Anyway, someone was mucking around with beeswax and accidentally made a new kind that, when you look through it, makes pollen all bright and glimmery. It's supposed to revolutionise (mum said that's like a new better way to do something) pollen collection. But I figure if it makes pollen collection easy then it will make pollen avoidance easy too. They are using the new wax to make these super cool wax-lens goggles and mum said I can get some.

April 5

Mum ordered the goggles today.

Can't wait!

April 6

Waiting for the goggles, watching mum clean, eating nectar.
Bored.

April 7 – April 17

Nothing new to report, still waiting for the goggles – apparently they are on backorder.

Been stuck inside, am so bored!

May 1

Still waiting. Mum says to stop checking the mail every two minutes.

May 9

Best day ever!

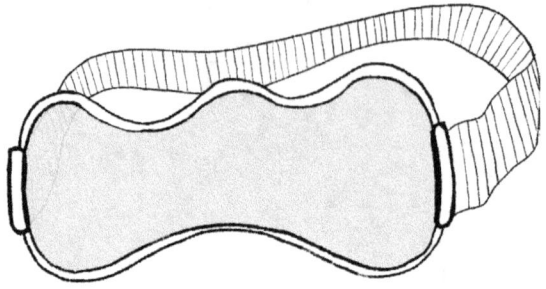

The goggles finally arrived and they are awesome.

I went everywhere. Had a couple of close calls but I managed to spin out of the way just in time to avoid airborne pollen. The goggles work great, they make the pollen kind of golden and shimmery so I can see all of it, even the tiny pieces.

I love flying.

I almost didn't get to go out. Mum was worried about me going out alone but she said I had waited so long it would be mean to make me wait until she had time to come with me. I had to promise not to take the goggles off and to be very careful.

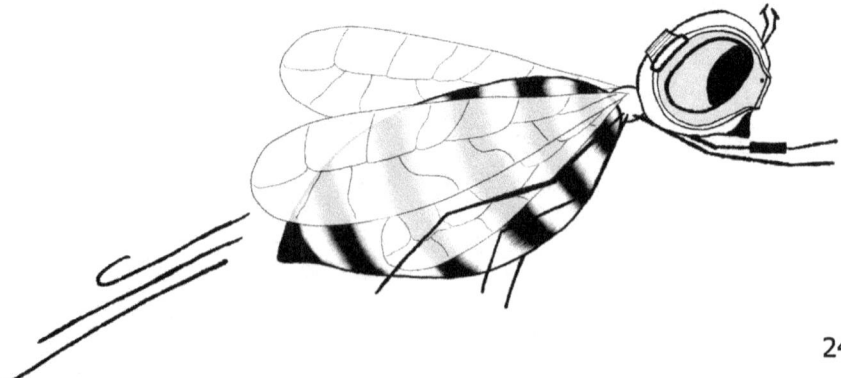

When I got home mum gave me a big hug and kept asking if I was OK. I didn't tell her my wings are aching but she knew - how does she always know stuff? – she suggested I take breaks to rest my wings when I go out tomorrow.

Cannot believe it, I was sure she would want me to stay home if I came back with any symptoms but apparently it's not from the pollen. Mum says I have sat around so much my muscles are out of practice so I need to go out every day to get them used to flying again.

May 10

Cannot wait until tomorrow. I am going to hang out with
Mazy, John, Inky, Link and Pip in the clover field and I am
going to teach them … something. I'm just not sure what.

It all happened when I was settling into a nice soft patch
of clover for a rest - when I got home I told mum it was
because she wanted me to take breaks but actually I was so
tired I felt like my wings were about to fall off. It was mega
windy today, pollen was going everywhere so I was flying
all over the place, spinning and looping and diving to stay
clear. I must have looked ridiculous.

Anyway, I didn't get much of a chance to relax, a group of
bees flew in and they were buzzing over the top of each
other at me.

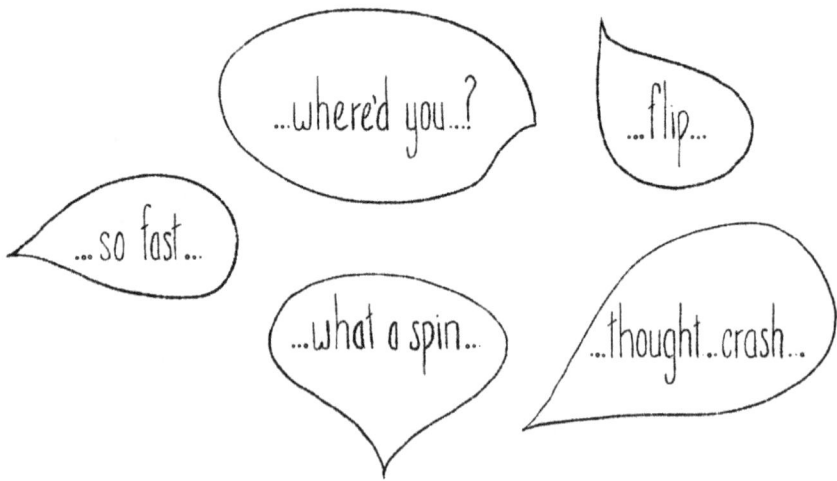

I think I must have looked a bit silly. I just sat there trying
to hide my tag and wishing I could get the goggles off. But

the other bees were nice enough not to comment on my weirdness and once they all calmed down Mazy asked if I could teach them some of my tricks.

I had no idea what tricks he was talking about. All I was doing was sitting on the ground but I said "yeah sure" with my wings crossed that they would either forget about it or I could figure out what was so special about how I was sitting on the clover.

They are all so cool and it would be great to hang out with them. I didn't want them to think I was weird and luckily none of them seemed to notice my tag.

Although it was a bit uncomfortable keeping my arm behind my head while we were talking. I'm hoping it looked like I was adjusting my goggle strap.

Will have to wear gloves or something tomorrow to hide my tag, I can't be adjusting the strap all the time.

Link — he said he likes my goggles - thought they were the latest in flying gear so I kind of just didn't tell him they are pollen goggles. Besides, they do help me fly - sort of.

Anyway, I told them I'm Ollie. We agreed to catch up again tomorrow for their lesson.

May 10 - really late

Can't sleep, a bit worried about seeing everyone tomorrow, am pretty sure they don't want to learn how to sit on the clover.

May 11 - really early

Exhausted, but I figured it out! It was my flying, they must have thought all that crazy pollen avoiding was trick-flying or something. They probably didn't even see the pollen because they didn't have my goggles on and some of it was miniscule specks. Now all I have to do is remember all the "tricks" I did so I can teach them.

May 11 - after dinner

I was so right. Mazy turned up wearing flying goggles - the old-fashioned kind designed for wind and sun glare - and the others wanted to know if they could still learn my flying tricks without them.

Nobody commented on my arm-warmer. I decided that would look cooler than gloves and I only needed to ask mum to make me one of those - don't think she would have made me six gloves in one night. In fact, I fitted in perfectly, the others were all wearing gloves and arm warmers too.

It was great, I showed them The dive, Flip Spin and Quick Dart – had to come up with some names for the moves to make it look official and technical. Couldn't call the moves "get out of the way of the drifting pollen above me", "avoid the spiralling whirly pollen patch" or "dodge the fast-moving updraft pollen".

A few times I had to do some creative flying to avoid pollen but I pretended I was working on new moves to teach them in the next lesson.

No new symptoms today, wings are still a bit stiff but mum says they will feel better in a few days. Had to have two serves of nectar tonight, so hungry.

May 12

Inky thinks we need to come up with a name for our flying club. I'm not sure we should, it makes me feel bad that I'm pretending to be this awesome flier. They don't know I am only doing the crazing flying tricks to avoid pollen and they are all completely accidental.

No new symptoms today.

May 13

Am kind of glad it rained today. My wings need a break and I can put off telling the flying group about my pollen allergy. Mum thinks I should tell them and I guess I agree. Hope they don't think I'm weird or tease me.

No new symptoms and my winds are feeling stronger than ever.

May 14

Today was a weird but great day and I am now an official member of the Free Flyers.

So I was flying super slow to meet everyone this morning, pretending I was enjoying the sunshine after the day inside. But if I am honest, I was delaying telling everyone about my pollen problem and not enjoying (or even noticing) the sunshine at all.

It's lucky the wind was lazy too, I'm not sure I would even have noticed pollen if it flew right into my face. Anyway, when I got to the clover field I was not surprised everyone beat me there but even in my distracted mood I could see something a little bizarre was going on.

Mazy was resting on a massive leaf. Link was pouring water over the clover. Then on the other side of Inky and John - who didn't appear to be doing anything unusual -, Pip was kind of flying upside down fanning the clover with his wings super fast. The poor clover was going all dry and shrivelled.

Unlucky for me he stirred up a tiny speck of pollen and it was coming right for me. I had to make a quick loop-spin-dive manoeuvre to miss it. Everyone stopped and stared at me.

I was sure they noticed my freak out about the pollen!

But no, that wasn't it, they had seen my tag reflecting in the sunlight – I guess I forgot my arm warmer this morning.

I was about to explain when they all started laughing and pulling off their gloves and arm-warmers. They all have tags too!

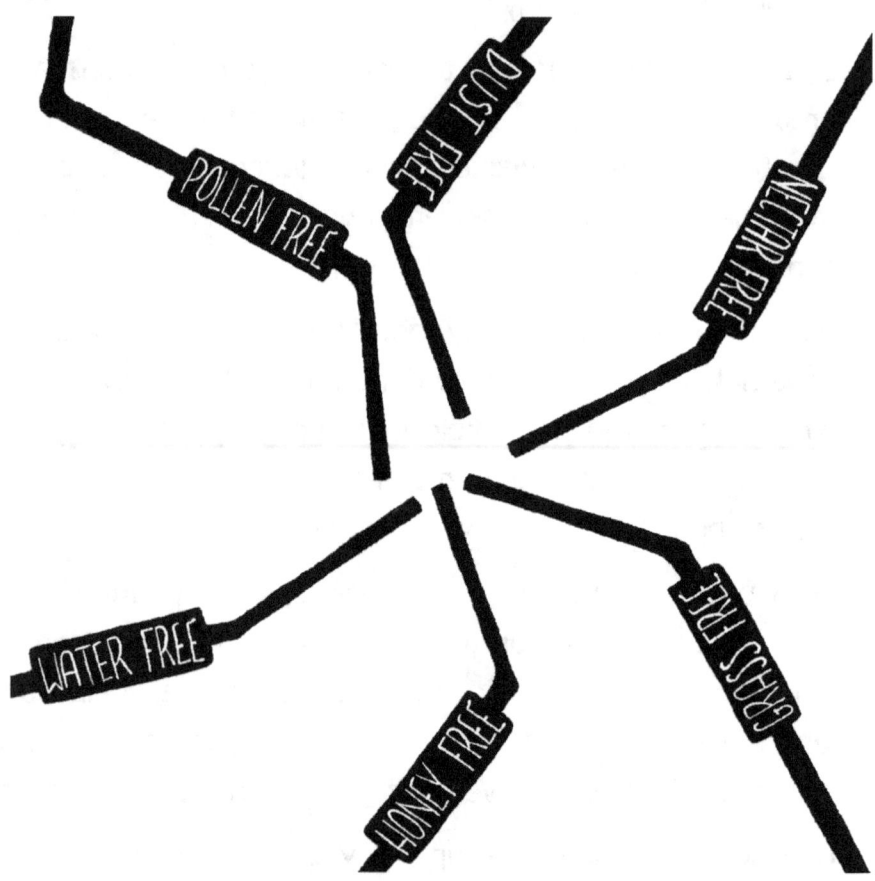

So it turns out they met each other at the Allergy and Intolerance Support Group. I have a pamphlet for it somewhere at home but the only snack they serve is pollen so mum said I couldn't join.

Mazy is "Grass Free" so he always finds a leaf or petal to sit on. Apparently, grass can poke up out of any ground even through clover.

John is "Nectar Free", he only eats pollen and honey. Its kind of handy for me, he is happy to be on pollen patrol any time and he even wants some Pollen Detection Goggles like mine so that snacks are super easy to find.

Inky is "Honey Free" which is tricky for his family as they work in the hive and have to decontaminate before they come into their compartment.

Link is "Dust Free" so he likes to keep a bottle of water with him to damp down any surfaces he is going to sit on. He needs to be careful around Pip who is "Water Free". This probably explains why Pip is the fastest flier of us all. His wings are super strong from all the drying he does with them.

We didn't do any flying practice today but we did name our club. Mazy suggested the Free Flyers and we all liked that name way better than my idea of calling us the IAF (Intolerant & Allergic Flyers).

Turns out they didn't want me to know about their allergies as much as I didn't want them to know about mine.

May 15

Hung out with the Free Flyers again today. Its, even more, fun now they know I am Pollen Free. We don't have to wear the arm-warmers and gloves anymore so we can try out some new cool tricks without our balance being thrown off with the clothing.

I was a little worried they wouldn't want me to teach them tricks anymore but they said I have skills and it doesn't matter that I invented them trying to avoid a sneezing fit.

Today we practised the Spinning Loop – kind of a fast spin while looping which is especially effective against scattering pollen - and the Back-Wing flip.

Pip came up with this one as a way to push the pollen away while flipping over it – he uses a version of this manoeuvre to avoid random drips of water.

May 16

Had a bit of an incident today. Mum had to take me to the doctor for an injection and decontamination. The pollen collector was right, that place is horrible and now I feel a bit bad I wasn't sympathetic to him when he had to decontaminate to take me outside.

Now I am home and mum is fussing. I guess the medicine she's giving me is helping with the puffiness but nothing seems to stop the sneezing and itching.

It all happened when I was practising a new trick, the Spinning Arrow - basically flying as fast as possible while spinning.

My goggles flipped off and I ended up flying straight into a massive pollen flurry. It was terrible, there was pollen everywhere and I couldn't escape.

John ate me free by snacking on a path of pollen to me but by then he and I were both covered in it so Mazy had to help me home. Inky came later with my goggles, mud splatter had glued them with petals, leaves and pollen. Apparently, the goggles took out some flowers before they landed in a muddy puddle.

Mum started buzzing again when she saw the state of my goggles. She seemed to calm down after I promised to be more careful and admitted that while it was an accident perhaps I have become a little too relaxed.

It's true, I had forgotten how bad I feel when pollen gets me. It was also a bit scary, I puffed up so much it was like stinger glue was all over my wings, I couldn't move them.

Anyway, she cleaned my goggles and made some adjustments so I can spin and flip and fly fast without them falling off. I think she is secretly happy that I have friends and am not stuck in the house all the time. This is despite the fact that she worries constantly and fusses at me to be careful and not to fly to far from medical attention.

New symptoms, I am nothing but symptoms today.

May 17

After all the drama yesterday we decided to spend the day in the clover field. I think everyone was a little freaked out but Mazy seemed especially unnerved. He said none of the leaves were big enough to protect him from the grass.

Most of the leaves in the clover patch were way bigger than him but he was so distressed we went on a leaf finding mission just to calm him down. John found a massive big lotus leaf near the lagoon which we all had to help carry over to the clover field.

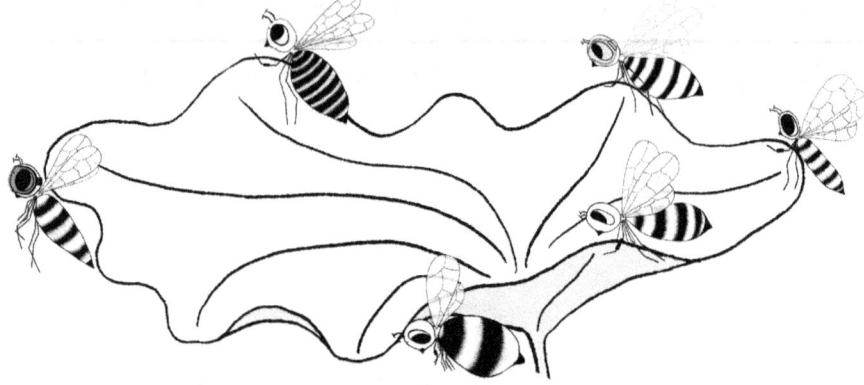

Symptoms today are OK, am still a little itchy but not too bad really considering the state I was in yesterday.

May 18

Had a funny feeling all day. At first, I thought it was the itch but no matter how much I scratched it didn't seem to help. It kept distracting my flying and I kept bumping into the others.

Mum says not to worry, she is sure the itch will be better soon.

May 19

OK, the itch is definitely gone, I didn't even have a sniffle last night but I had that funny feeling again when I went outside. Hope I am not getting a new allergy to sunshine or anything like that. Mum says it's not likely but to keep track of my eating, activities and symptoms just in case.

Had a little honey mixed with my nectar for dinner tonight, it was nice for a change. No new symptoms.

May 20

This is getting ridiculous, whenever I am out with the Free
Flyers I feel all twitchy. I'm starting to think there is
somebody watching me but whenever I turn around all I
see is the garden and stray bits of sparkly pollen to avoid.

No new symptoms, nectar for breakfast, lunch and dinner
as usual.

May 21

Mystery solved!

I was right, there is somebody spying on me, well on the Free Flyers actually. His name is Flynn and I caught him hiding in the clover patch watching the group flying in formation. I was practising a new Duck and Dive trick – I think this one might come in handy for sneaky pollen that is swirling - and just as I ducked I spotted Flynn.

Anyway, I adjusted my dive to come in behind him. He didn't notice me there and I heard him muttering something about flying, tags and friends. I was starting to feel bad about listening in on what were undoubtedly private thoughts so I did a little greeting buzz.

I must have given him quite a shock. As he zoomed away he forgot to flap his wings and face planted on the ground. I helped him up and introduced myself. No sooner had he said "I'm Flynn" than he was off again - this time remembering to flap – I didn't even get a chance to ask him if he wanted to practice flying with us.

May 22

The Free Flyers had a special mission today, we wanted to find Flynn and ask him to fly with us – I think he could use the help, he seems kind of erratic out of control - but I told the others it's because he seemed nice, which is also true.

I finally found him sitting in the middle of a flower, covered in pollen so I could only yell from a distance. He probably thinks I'm weird now which explains why he said he wouldn't fit in with our group when I called out to him to come fly with us.

I talked to mum about Flynn tonight, she thinks we should try again. He might be nervous to join such a big group of friends or may not have heard me right seeing as I was so far away. She did suggest that if he is covered in pollen again that I get one of the others to talk to him, she really doesn't want another pollen incident any time soon.

May 23

Spent the morning with the Free Flyers practising the Tuck and Roll. We have so many moves now I might have to make a special book to remember them all.

No sign of Flynn.

May 24

Finally figured out what's going on with Flynn. I spotted him again, this time thankfully he was pollen free. He tried to fly off but I am pretty fast these days – all the flying practice has definitely improved my speed and stamina - and apparently, my pollen evading tricks are useful for catching bees too.

Flynn was pretty impressed I could catch him but he was also a little annoyed with me for not leaving him alone like he wanted. This didn't make any sense to me, I had firsthand experience of being alone and it was miserable. He said he wasn't like the rest of us, couldn't fly like us, didn't have one of our cool tags and liked keeping to himself.

My tag is so not cool. I don't hide it anymore, but still, to wish you had one seemed strange to me. I had to explain to Flynn about my Pollen Allergy and that if I get sick the tag will let anyone know to take me to the doctor for anti-pollen treatment.

So weird, Flynn still seems to wish he had a tag – not sure he really gets that we all wish we didn't need tags – but he seems to think that without a tag he can't be part of our flying group.

Symptoms, nothing new to report.

May 25

The Free Flyers have a new member today, Flynn.

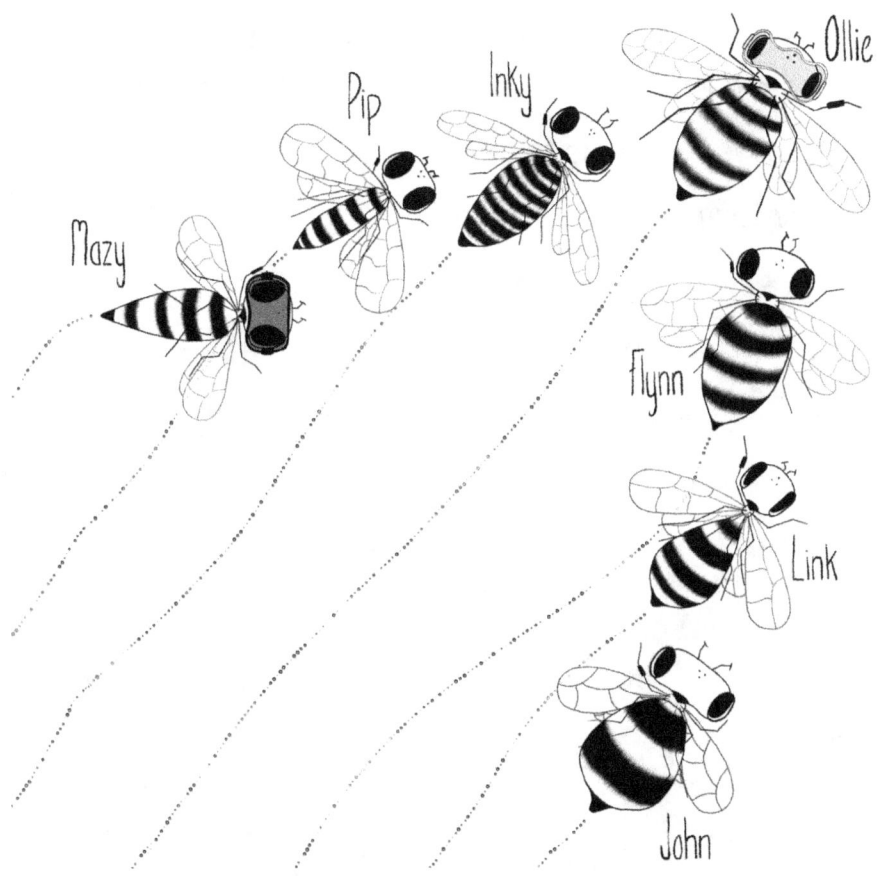

He has a brand new tag – mum helped me make it last night – it says "Allergy Free". It means he has no allergies or intolerances but likes to fly.

Lucky Flynn likes flying so much, he needs lots of practice. Am wondering if we should have made his tag "Fear Free".

He totally tries to do all our hardest tricks without any training and usually ends up crashing into someone else or the ground.

He is also a great help in keeping a lookout for stray nectar, water, dust, grass, honey, pollen and at telling jokes.

We have a new motto too.

Flying free as me!